A

JUST-RIGHT
leveled readers

P9-CWD-542

That Cat

An Animal Friends Reader

by Liza Charlesworth
illustrated by Ian Smith

ISBN: 978-0-545-85970-7

10 9 8 7 6 5 4 3 2 1   15 16 17 18 19/0

Printed in the U.S.A.   40
First printing 2015

Book design by Maria Mercado

SCHOLASTIC INC.

That cat can walk!

That cat can talk!

That cat can hide!

That cat can ride!

That cat can sweep!

That cat can leap!

That cat can throw!

That cat can sew!

That cat can spin!

That cat can win!

That cat can do anything!

Comprehension Boosters

1. Is this story real or pretend? How do you know?

2. What is your favorite thing this cat can do? Why?

3. Would you like to have a cat like this? Why or why not?